Mary Y. Spitz

Mint's Christmas Message

drawings by
Joanne Y. Pierce

Mother Moose Press
Potomac Falls Virginia

*MERRY CHRISTMAS TO THE BALSAM FAMILY!
love, Mary*

Printed in the United States of America
First Edition

Edited by Susan Wejchert and Janet Jermott
Book Design by Tom and Mary Spitz

ISBN 0-9724570-0-3

Library of Congress Control Number: 2002114174

Mother Moose Press
PMB #435
21010 Southbank Street
Potomac Falls, VA 20165

To Rebecca, Tom, my parents, family, friends, MLS, and Mint.
— Mary Y. Spitz

To Tom, Marie, Steve, my parents, family, friends, and to God.
(Proverbs 16:3)
— Joanne Y. Pierce

A Special Dedication:

To my husband's father, the Rev. Dr. C. Thomas Spitz, Jr.

Many years ago, Dr. Spitz gave a sermon that touched my husband so deeply that he spoke of it often. In the sermon, he told a story about a man and his attempts on Christmas Eve to help a flock of birds. One Christmas, as a gift to my husband and with the sermon in mind, I wrote this story.

I would like to dedicate this book to the many sermons given each week that help guide us through life.

— MYS

In our small town of Port Washington, just off Main Street, is Lisa Lane. If you take Lisa Lane north and make the first left you would be on Heritage Farm Road. Looking to your right you will see the Herman's Horse Farm. During the Christmas season it is hard to miss, for there are many holiday decorations adorning the old place. One of the favorites among the children in town is the red tractor with the Christmas lights and wreaths in the wheels.

But the best part about Christmas on the Herman's Horse Farm is a special pony who does not mind wearing a Santa hat. Grandpa Tom, who owns the farm, gave this pony to his granddaughter Rebecca on her sixth Christmas. It is one of the only Christmas gifts he ever gave. The pony's name is Mint.

Mint is now an old pony—thirty years old, to be exact. Rebecca, now all grown up, lives down the road and visits Mint almost every day with her children. Mint is wonderful with children.

Grandpa Tom would always say, "A kind-hearted pony is worth more than his weight in gold."

And Grandpa Tom should know, because he trained horses and ponies for a living. Some of his animals even turned out to be champions, including Mint.

In our town, Mint has a special place in all of our hearts, but none as special as in Grandpa Tom's heart. There is a Christmas Eve story that is told every year here in Port. It involves ol' Grandpa Tom, some nasty December weather, some Christmas spirit, and Mint the pony.

The first thing you have to know is that Grandpa Tom did not think very highly of Christmas and all that came with it. He rarely helped with the decorations, the baking, or the shopping. It was Grandma Jane who drove the sleigh for the Christmas caroling hay ride. Grandpa Tom wanted no part of it.

Now, as I recall, that Christmas season started as all the others did. The only difference was the rash of harsh December snowstorms. The worst storm yet was forecast for Christmas Eve. As usual, this time of year, there was a bit of a storm going on inside the house too. In fact, by the time Christmas Eve arrived, there were so many holiday activities going on that Grandpa Tom had to escape to his favorite room in the attic that overlooked the farm.

Grandpa Tom made it well known that he did not allow Christmas decorations in his attic room. So it was there, with his pipe, his book, and a hot cup of tea that he sat gazing out at the falling snow in what he thought was peace.

As she did each year, Grandma Jane walked up the stairs and asked: "Would you like to come to the afternoon Christmas Eve service?"

And he answered as he did each year: "No thank you, Jane."

With the family gone, Grandpa Tom was enjoying the quiet, his pipe, his book, and his cup of tea. But looking out the window he noticed that in the field Mint and the other horses were standing huddled together and not eating their hay. He felt that the winter blankets and field sheds were enough shelter for most conditions, but with the weather turning particularly harsh he started to become concerned.

"Some of those horses do not have strong winter coats," he thought. "The wind has picked up, the snow is falling harder, and they've stopped eating."

Without hesitation he got up, went downstairs, put on his coat, boots, hat, and gloves and ran to the field to get the horses into the barn and out of the weather.

When he got to the field, though, a strange thing happened. None of the horses came when he called. He walked toward Mint, but as he got close, Mint ran away.

"Now is not the time to act like a two year old, my friend. Ho!" he said. Mint halted, but as soon as Grandpa Tom got close to him, he ran away again.

"Mint, I am in no mood to chase an old pony around a field in a snowstorm. We are both too old for such games. Ho!" Mint halted. This time, when Grandpa Tom got close, he reared and ran away.

"Has this snow frozen your brain?" he asked. "Well fine, I'll just get the others first and you had better follow." So, he headed toward Sunny. But as he was about to place the halter on his head, Sunny ran away too.

"What the heck is darn tooting going on around here?" he thought to himself. As he walked toward each of the animals, Mr. Whipple, Shadow, Ollie, Chee Chee, and Worthy, they all ran away. Any other day, he would just have let them all stay out, but he knew the storm was becoming too fierce for Mint, and Grandpa Tom really started to worry.

"These horses always come when I call. This has never happened before," he thought. "Well," he said aloud, "desperate times call for desperate measures."

He went into the feed room and got some carrots and a bucket of sweet feed. He walked back outside and banged the bucket and shook the bag of carrots. Normally, they all would have come at a gallop, but this time they just looked at him, then turned away. Not one came running.

Grandpa Tom took a deep breath and rubbed his head. He had used every trick in an old horse trainer's book to get those animals through the gate and into the barn. Nothing had worked.

By this time, the snow had changed to freezing rain. Ice covered Mint's tail and mane. His winter blanket had soaked through and he was starting to shiver. Even so, each time Grandpa Tom tried to go near icy Mint, he ran away.

Getting cold and tired himself, Grandpa Tom was near panic. What will become of that old stubborn pony? What would he tell the children? What would he tell Rebecca? He could not understand why the animals were not accepting his help.

His panic was so bad he too started to shiver. Then he noticed Mint lying down in the snow. His panic turned into a deep sadness and he started to cry.

He walked over to Mint. Mint lifted his head to look at him. As Grandpa Tom knelt over him he whispered, "If only I were a pony, one of you, even for a little while, I'd be able to communicate with you, lead you to safety, and take away your coldness and pain."

As he knelt over the freezing pony his thoughts went to Christmas Eve and his family. He wondered how something like this could happen on this day. But something was nagging at him. A thought that he couldn't shake. That thought led to another and soon a flood of feelings and insight consumed him. Christmas, he pondered, the day God's son came to this earth as a baby. A baby who would one day be able to communicate with people, to be one of them, to talk to them, to show them the way to safety, and to take away their pain.

A wave of understanding and clarity about the meaning of Christmas consumed him. "I never understood it before," he whispered. "As I kneel here wishing I were a pony, God's wish was to become human for the same purpose—to communicate, to save. The Savior. I understand."

As he spoke the last word, Mint stood up and looked right into Grandpa Tom's eyes, just as Grandpa Tom had looked into Mint's as he trained him long ago.

Mint proceeded to walk through the gate, into the barn and into his stall of soft bedding and warmth. The other horses allowed Grandpa Tom to lead them into the barn, all eyeing him with the same intensity as Mint.

With happiness in his heart, Grandpa Tom went into the stalls and replaced the icy blankets with dry stable blankets. Then he gave them oats, carrots, hay, and loving pats on their necks.

The next thing he did is what made the ol' grump the talk of the town. Grandpa Tom started up the red tractor, the one with the Christmas lights and the wreaths in the wheels. He drove that tractor down Heritage Farm Road, down Lisa Lane, down Main Street, and turned right into the church parking lot.

For the first time in many, many years, Grandpa Tom walked up the church stairs, opened the doors and stepped inside. He walked up two rows and stood with his hand on Grandma Jane's shoulder. Even with the singing, the bells, and the organ, Grandpa Tom was at peace.

Grandpa Tom looked up and gave thanks for the wonder of Christmas. Then he gave special thanks for the Christmas Day he gave his granddaughter Rebecca a pony . . .

. . . a pony named Mint.